ALIEN BRAIN FRYOUT

A Wild Willie Mystery

More Wild Willie Mysteries
by Barbara M. Joosse

Wild Willie and King Kyle Detectives

The Losers Fight Back

Ghost Trap

Barbara M. Joosse

ALIEN BRAIN
FRYOUT

A Wild Willie Mystery

Illustrated by Sue Truesdell

Clarion Books
New York

Clarion Books
a Houghton Mifflin Company imprint
215 Park Avenue South, New York, NY 10003
Text copyright © 2000 by Barbara M. Joosse
Illustrations copyright © 2000 by Sue Truesdell

The text for this book was set in 14-point Palatino.
The illustrations were executed in pen and ink with ink washes
on Arches cold-press watercolor paper.

Printed in the U.S.A.

Library of Congress Cataloging-in-Publication Data

Joosse, Barbara M.
Alien brain fryout : a Wild Willie Mystery /
by Barbara M. Joosse ; illustrated by Sue Truesdell.
p. cm.
Summary: When the neighborhood bully starts following Willie, Lucy,
and Kyle around and acting goofy, they suspect that he's been abducted
by aliens until Scarface the parrot presents another possibility.
ISBN 0-395-68964-3
[1. Bullies—Fiction. 2. Detectives—Fiction. 3. Extraterrestrial beings—
Fiction. 4. Friendship—Fiction.] I. Truesdell, Sue, ill. II. Title.

PZ7.J7435 A1 2000
[Fic]—dc21

99-086359

VB 10 9 8 7 6 5 4 3 2

To Tim,
you're getting closer
—B. J.

To Alex with love
—S.T.

Contents

◆ 1 ◆

Headquarters

My partners and I were fooling around with Kyle's Magic Eight Ball. I was holding it. "Magic Eight Ball," I chanted. "Are we the best detective agency in the universe?"

I shook the ball and waited for the answer to float up. Reply hazy. Try again.

Lucy grabbed the ball. "My turn. Magic Eight Ball, am I the best detective on the team?"

Lucy shook the ball . . . hard. The answer floated up. Reply hazy. Try again.

She said, "Is this ball broken, or what? It's stuck on the same answer."

Kyle grabbed the ball from Lucy. "That's because you're not asking the right questions. You have to ask better questions. Like this . . . Magic Eight Ball, should we get headquarters?"

That *was* a pretty good question. We all stared at the little glass window and waited for the answer. It floated up. Yes.

Scarface flew over to Kyle's shoulder. *"Braaack! Move it, baby."*

Did I mention Scarface? He's our mascot, an African Grey parrot. He can say a million words, most of which he learned from watching cop shows with his previous owner, Loraine Lamonde, a.k.a. Loony Loraine.

Did I mention Loony Loraine? She was an amateur detective who used to own this house. Scarface was her parrot.

"The Magic Eight Ball knows all," said Kyle. "It knows we need headquarters."

"Yeah," said Lucy. "How can we be a real detective agency without headquarters?"

"But where should we have it?" Kyle asked.

"My house," said Lucy. "I have lots of disguise stuff."

"My house," I said. "I have lots of food."

"Loraine, Loraine!" said Scarface.

Lucy said, "Scarface has a point. This *is* a pretty creepy house. Loony Loraine died here, and there's a secret passage."

"Plus all her old detective stuff is stored in the attic," said Kyle.

"YES!" I yelled. "Let's set up headquarters in the attic!"

Kyle shook up the Magic Eight Ball and waited for the answer. Yes, definitely.

It took about two seconds to run up the stairs, into Kyle's room, through the secret passage in his closet, and up the stairs to the creepiest attic you ever saw. It took another two seconds to start moving things around.

"Let's put the file cabinet next to the desk, just the way Loraine used to have it in her living room," said Kyle.

"I think we should have *everything* the way Loraine had it—this *is* her stuff," said Lucy.

Lucy and I shoved the bulletin board behind the desk. Kyle stuffed the file drawers full of Loraine's investigation reports. I put the Magic Eight Ball and copies of *Detective* and *Alert!* magazines on the table. Lucy plugged in the TV and we all shoved

the sofa in front. Scarface flew around the attic screeching, *"Gotcha, baby!"* and *"Police!"* and *"You're surrounded!"*

"We're all set," Kyle said. "We have every single thing we need for detective work."

"Everything except a case," said Lucy.

"We've put posters all over the neighborhood, but nobody's called," I said. "I guess there haven't been any disappearances or robberies lately."

Kyle slumped down on the sofa. "Here we've got everything ready for a case, and crime hits the skids."

Scarface flew to Kyle's shoulder and stroked his hair with his beak. *"Awww! Whatsa matter, baby?"*

"C'mon, guys. Cheer up," said Lucy. "Crime is all around us. We just have to find it."

"Lucy's right," I said. "Grafton is probably crawling with bad guys."

"Yeah, maybe they're just hiding," said

Kyle. "So how are we going to find them?"

"Surveillance," said Lucy. "We watch for weird stuff and take notes. Then we figure things out . . . and nab the bad guys."

"Exactly," I said, looking at my watch. "Only now it's time for our favorite TV show. We'll have to find crime when the show's over."

We turned on the tube and squinched together on the sofa—Lucy, Kyle, Scarface, and me, Wild Willie. Our favorite show, *Alien,* was about how aliens abduct people and then return them to Earth. Only when the people come back, they act spacey and strange, like aliens are controlling their minds. Sometimes aliens do other creepy things. In this episode they filled the sewers with giant tapeworms that crept through the pipes into toilets and sinks and took over people's bodies. We watched as the worms squirmed under people's skin. We watched as people got

weird because of the worms living in their bodies. We watched as people puked them out and the worms slithered back into the sewers . . . where they waited for their next victims.

"Yowzer!" I said. "It sure would be creepy to have those giant worms in your body."

"Aliens have lots of ways to gain control," Lucy said.

"*Watch out!*" screamed Scarface.

I peeked through the attic window. "You know, aliens could be watching us right now," I said.

"There could be people in Grafton who've been abducted," Kyle said. "Maybe even in Sunset Court." He looked around suspiciously.

It gave me the creeps to think about it. I think it creeped out Kyle and Lucy, too, because headquarters became very quiet.

Very, very quiet.

Then Kyle's Mom yelled up to us. "It's time for Lucy and Willie to go home."

Yowzer!

Lucy and I said good-bye to Kyle and Scarface and walked outside. Just the two of us. In the dark.

◆ 2 ◆

Strange Behavior

Have you ever noticed how things are weirder at night? Tonight the sky was black and the full moon was floating in it like an eyeball. Sounds are creepier at night, too. There are more owls hooting and dogs barking. There are more footsteps. There are more leaves rustling.

Like right now, I thought I heard whispering. Where was it coming from?

And those footsteps. Were they just walking-down-the-street footsteps, or

were they I'm-coming-to-get-you foot-steps?

Pop!

I grabbed Lucy's arm.

"What was that noise?" whispered Lucy.

"Maybe somebody shooting off fire-crackers."

"Right," said Lucy. "I'm sure a spaceship backfiring would sound a lot sharper."

"Right," I said.

Zzzhoooooosh.

Lucy grabbed my arm. "Th-th-that didn't sound anything like a giant sewer worm," she said. "D-d-did it?"

"I don't think so," I said.

Zzzhoooooosh.

"But maybe we should walk on the other side of the sidewalk—away from the sewer grates."

"Do you think Kyle is right?" Lucy asked. "Do you think aliens could be in Sunset Court?"

"Aliens are very sneaky," I said. "You never know when they'll attack, or even who they are."

"Then who can you trust?" Lucy asked.

"You know what they say on *Alien*," I said. "Trust no one."

"Except your partners," Lucy said.

"Right," I said. "We can definitely count on each other."

Which is when I noticed our shadows in the street lights. Our shadows were not very big. *We* weren't very big. I knew I could count on Lucy; I just wish there was more of her to count on.

"So how do you know if somebody's been abducted?" I squeaked.

"Well, they act like the guys on the show. Dopey. Jumpy. Not like their regular selves," Lucy said.

"Everybody I know is acting regular," I said. "So far."

That's when I had this weird feeling,

like somebody was watching us. But then I thought I was probably only creeped out about the TV show. Probably no one was really watching.

But I kept having that feeling. I stopped walking and looked over my shoulder. Lucy and I were the only people on the sidewalk. If somebody was watching us, and we couldn't see them . . . that meant they were hiding!

Then I heard *breathing*.

Suddenly, there were footsteps coming after us! We ran. The footsteps ran!

I could see my house. We were almost there. A few more steps and . . .

. . . we made it! Lucy and I ran inside, slammed the door, bolted it, and dove behind the sofa.

"Hello, there," said Dad.

"Dad!" I cried.

"What's the problem?" he asked.

I swallowed. "Aliens," I said.

"Or abductees," said Lucy. "We don't know which."

"Something was chasing you?" asked Dad.

We nodded.

"Well, let's just have a look," said Dad, reaching for the curtains to open them.

"NO!" we cried. "Don't let it see you!"

"Of course," said Dad, slapping his forehead. "I don't know why I didn't think of that. I guess that's why you're the detectives and I'm the banker."

"You *could* look through a tiny slit in the curtains," suggested Lucy.

"Naturally," said Dad. He crouched down and opened the curtains a crack. Slowly, slowly he peeked out the window. "Well, what do you know," he said, shaking his head.

"What is it?" I asked.

"It isn't an alien at all," said Dad. "It's Chuckie."

"Same thing," said Lucy.

We peeked under the curtains. There was big, mean, rotten Chuckie staring at my house. The streetlight and the eyeball moon were making him look creepier than ever. "This is very bad," I said.

"Why did Chuckie follow us? Why's he standing there?" Lucy said.

"Chuckie is an unusual young man," said Dad. "But I'm sure he doesn't mean any harm."

"Yeah, right," said Lucy under her breath.

We went into the kitchen and opened up the snack cupboard. We got out Cheese-Whizzier Corn Chips, salted peanuts-in-a-shell (my favorite), black licorice, and Star Zonkers. We spread them out on the table.

"You do have the best food," said Lucy.

"I know," I said.

Lucy ate one chip, one bite of licorice, one peanut, and one Zonker. Then she started over again. "Your dad's kind of dumb for a smart guy," she said. "He thinks Chuckie's nice."

"There are two kinds of grownups," I said. "The kind who think all kids are cute, and the kind who think all kids are rotten. Dad's the first kind."

"Maybe Chuckie wouldn't be so bad if he wasn't so big," Lucy said.

"Yeah. He's so big he can pound any-body he wants to," I said.

"Maybe he wouldn't be so bad if he didn't like money so much."

"Right. He's always trying to trick us out of ours."

"And he wouldn't be so bad if he didn't hate work."

"Since he's always trying to get us to do his."

"Maybe he wouldn't seem so rotten if we were smarter," said Lucy. "Then he couldn't trick us."

"The trouble is, we get smarter, but he keeps getting trickier. Let's face it. Dad's dead wrong. Chuckie's the rottenest kid we know."

"Why do you think he was following us?" asked Lucy.

"Maybe it's the full moon," I said. "People get weird when there's a full moon."

Lucy looked out of the window. "The moon *is* full," she said. "Maybe Chuckie followed us because of the full moon, and then tomorrow the moon won't be full and everything will be back to normal."

"Right," I said.

◆ 3 ◆

Surveillance

In the morning, everything was regular. The sun was shining and it was summer-hot. Dad put a load of laundry in the washer before he left for work. Mom made me eat breakfast. I didn't feel eyes watching me. Nobody was chasing me. Regular.

I was just about to walk out of my front door when I saw Chuckie. He was standing across the street, looking . . . not regular. He was standing there, not doing anything! He had this dopey look on his face, like people have when they first wake up, and he was looking at Lucy's house. I didn't want him to see me, so instead of going out the front door, I climbed out my window, snuck through the hole in the hedge, and threw stones at Lucy's bedroom window.

The window opened. By itself. I didn't see Lucy anywhere. A voice said, "Come in."

I climbed in and almost fell on top of Lucy. She was crouched under the window. "What are you doing down there?" I asked.

"Hiding," she said. "From Chuckie."

"What's he doing on the sidewalk?" I asked.

"I don't know," Lucy said. "But he's been standing there all morning, just watching my house."

"Why would Chuckie be watching your house? There isn't a full moon now. There isn't even *any* moon!" I said.

"I told you, I don't know. But he's giving me the creeps."

"Chuckie always gives me the creeps, but this time is different," I said. "Usually he's trying to trick us, but now . . . "

"Maybe that's it! Maybe he's got a scheme. This is the watching-us part, and then comes the getting-us part."

"Maybe . . . " I said.

"You know what's wrong?" Lucy said.

"We can't figure out what's up with Chuckie because we don't have enough information. We have to do some surveillance."

Lucy's got a whole box of disguises and two shelves of spy equipment . . . including a periscope. She snuck the periscope in front of the window and watched Chuckie with it. I took notes.

"The subject is a ten-year-old male," she said. "He's wearing motorcycle boots, shorts, and a T-shirt. He appears to have changed his hairstyle. It isn't spiky, it's combed."

"What's he doing?" I asked.

"The subject has been standing in the same spot for two hours. He isn't doing anything. He's just standing there.

"That's it," said Lucy, pulling down the periscope. "There isn't any more to observe."

"Okay," I said. "Then let's interrogate him. Maybe we can get him to say what he wants from us."

We walked out the front door and crossed the street. "Hi, Chuckie," Lucy said.

"Oh, hi!" Chuckie said in a voice that didn't sound like his.

"Man, oh man!" I said, yawning. "A

25

whole day with nothing to do. Nope. I don't have any work at all."

"Neither do I," Lucy said.

Here's where Chuckie usually would have an idea. Here's where he'd give us a chance to learn all about plants . . . by weeding his family's vegetable garden. But Chuckie didn't say anything. He just stood there. Grinning.

If he didn't want us to work for him, maybe he wanted our money. I nudged Lucy.

"I just got my allowance," Lucy said. "And I don't have a single thing to spend it on."

Chuckie just grinned.

"Yup," Lucy said. "Me with all that money and not a single idea of how to spend it."

"Maybe you should buy some earrings," he said.

I squinted my eyes at the Chuckster.

"Why? Do you have some earrings you want Lucy to buy? Like maybe real diamonds that cost the exact price of her allowance?"

"No," Chuckie said. "I just thought she'd look nice in some earrings."

Huh?

Lucy said, "Chuckie, you've been standing out here a long time. How come?"

"I was, uh, well, I was meditating."

Chuckie, *meditating???*

"You'd better meditate in the shade, then, Chuckie," Lucy said. "Your face is getting really red."

◆ 4 ◆

Aaaaaugh!

Lucy and I rode our bikes to Kyle's house. There was Kyle, playing with Scarface.

"We have a case!" I said.

"Let's get to headquarters," said Kyle, and we raced up the stairs.

"It started last night," said Lucy. "Willie and I were walking home, and we had this feeling like somebody was watching us. Somebody was."

"We walked fast, and he walked faster. We ran, and he ran, too," I said.

Scarface leaned forward on Kyle's

shoulder like he was listening hard and could actually understand what we were saying.

"When we got to Willie's house, we looked back outside. You'll never guess who it was," said Lucy. She waited a second before she sprang it on him. "Chuckie."

"*Aaaaaugh!*" screamed Scarface, his feathers standing out like spikes.

Kyle started petting Scarface to calm him down. "Chuckie was probably trying to trick you," said Kyle. "Get money out of you or something. You know how he is."

"We thought of that. But he's not acting like his regular money-grubbing self. This morning he stood across the street and just stared at my house. We decided to observe him and try to figure out why," Lucy said.

"Then we interrogated him. We said

we didn't have any work to do . . . but he didn't try to get us to do his," I said.

"And then I said I'd just gotten my allowance and didn't have anything to spend it on . . . but he didn't try to get it," Lucy said.

"*Veeeery interesting,*" said Scarface.

"Exactly," said Lucy.

Kyle rubbed his hands together. "Sounds like a case." He got up. "Okay. Let's list all the things about Chuckie—the way he was before and the way he is now."

He wrote down *Chuckie—Before.* We started listing things, and here's what we came up with.

Chuckie-Before
1. Big
2. Dressed like tough guy
3. Spiky hair
4. Liked money
5. Hated work
6. Tried to trick us
7. Looked sneaky / smart
8. Called us losers
9. Sat around on his porch

"Now let's start the other list, the way he is now," said Lucy.

That list looked like this:

Chuckie-Now
1. Big
2. Dresses like tough guy
3. Combed hair
4. Likes money . . . ?
5. Hates work . . . ?
6. Hasn't tried to trick us lately
7. Looks dopey
8. Followed Willie and Lucy
9. Stared at Lucy's house

"Something else I noticed," said Lucy. "His face is really red, like he's been in the sun too long."

Kyle wrote down:

10. Red face

"I know what you're thinking," said

Kyle. "You're thinking the aliens got Chuckie. That he was abducted and maybe now they control his mind."

Lucy and I nodded.

"Maybe," said Kyle. "And maybe not.

I'll admit, it sounds like Chuckie's acting weird. But the only thing smarter and sneakier than aliens is Chuckie. He could just have some big scheme."

"But he wasn't acting smart," said Lucy.

"He was acting like a piece of his brain was missing."

"Like he had brain fryout," I said.

I picked up the Magic Eight Ball and started fooling around with it. I tipped it over. The message in the window was this: Signs point to yes.

Mwiiip!

Kyle opened up a copy of *Alert!*, a magazine about aliens. He flipped through pages of guys with skinny bodies and big heads (aliens) and humans with zombie eyes (abductees). He thumped his finger on one of the pages. "Look at this," he said. "A description of different kinds of alien control."

"Yow!" I said. "Lemme see."

Lucy and I looked at the article.

"It says there are lots of ways aliens can

gain control of you," I said. "You can get beamed up into a spaceship. Surgery. Telepathy. Computer chip implants. Stuff like that."

"Computer implants!" Lucy said. "Maybe that's Chuckie's scam. He'd sell me earrings with computer chips inside. Then aliens would control my mind."

"It could happen," Kyle said. He read out loud. "'When under mind control, victims may act in a manner very different from their usual behavior.'"

"Like Chuckie's brain fryout," Lucy said.

Kyle read on. "'Sometimes a victim's appearance even changes.'"

"Chuckie sure looks different," I said. "His face is clean, and he's gelled his hair."

Lucy grabbed the magazine and read more. "'Abduction victims are often afraid of bright lights, most likely because they remind them of the lights on a spaceship.'"

"That makes sense." I looked over Lucy's shoulder. "'Victims are also afraid of loud noises like airplane engines, probably because it reminds them of the sound of a landing spaceship.'

"And look what it says at the end of the article!" I cried. "'Victims are a great danger to themselves and others. They should be watched carefully. Authorities should be notified.' Then they underline this part. 'Do not (repeat: DO NOT) take any action without proper authorization.'"

"Who *are* the authorities?" Lucy asked.

I tapped the magazine. "*Alert!*, of course. They know everything about alien control."

"Then let's write and tell them about Chuckie. We can send in reports as we do our investigation," said Kyle.

We wrote the letter.

REPORT #1

Dear Alert!,

Chuckie Herman is a kid in our neighborhood. He's usually mean and tricky, but now he's acting dopey. It's like he has brain fryout. He looks different, too. His hair is usually spiky, and now it's gelled down. Also, his face is red.

We'll keep you posted.

Detectively yours,
Scarface Detectives

"Okay. We've notified the authorities. Now it's time to spy on Chuckie," Lucy said.

We got our notebook, the periscope, and the binoculars. Then Kyle rubbed Scarface's head good-bye.

Scarface started bobbing up and down, and then he made a noise, a weird one. It sounded like this: *Mwiiip.*

41

"What was that?" Lucy said. "A parrot sneeze?"

"I don't know," said Kyle. "But he's been doing that a lot lately."

"He probably has a cold," I said.

"*Mwiiip,*" said Scarface.

6

Computer Chips

Lucy and I watched Chuckie's house with our bare eyeballs. Kyle hogged the binoculars. The binoculars were his.

"I can't see a single thing with my plain eyes," said Lucy. "Just Chuckie's dumb house."

I sighed. "Yup. You can't see much without binoculars."

"That's true," said Kyle. "With the binoculars I can see all kinds of stuff. There's dish soap on the kitchen window

sill. There's kind of a blue light coming from the living room . . ."

"An *alien light?*" Lucy asked.

"More like a TV light," said Kyle.

"What else?" Lucy asked.

"Wow! There's a whole green and yellow room with the most Packer football stuff you ever saw! A giant Superbowl Champions banner and a neon *Run with the Pack* light. But not Chuckie. He must not be home."

"Can I look through the binoculars?" Lucy asked.

"I don't know," Kyle said. "These lenses are glass. They could break real easy."

"I'll be careful."

"You could drop them."

"I won't."

"You might."

Lucy's eyes got skinny. "Kyle," she said. "If we're partners, then we share. Even-steven. We share work. We share notes. We share binoculars."

"If they break . . ."

Suddenly, I saw something moving at Chuckie's. What was it?

". . . then you have to pay for them," said Kyle.

Chuckie's front door swung open.

"Over my dead body," snapped Lucy.

I jabbed Lucy and Kyle with my elbows.

"Huh?" they said.

I pointed to the front door. Chuckie was coming through it. He was carrying something. He was walking right to our hiding place.

"Hi, guys," he said. "Whatcha doing?"

"Hi," I said. "Uh. We're looking for . . ."

". . . tent caterpillars. They can do a lot of damage to your bushes, you know," Kyle said.

"I know," said Chuckie. "But how come you've got binoculars?"

The binoculars did look pretty suspicious. How were we going to get out of this? Just then, the town's noon whistle blew.

"Lunch time," said Lucy. "My mom really gets mad when I'm late for lunch. We'd better go, Chuckie. See you."

Chuckie picked up Lucy's sweater. "Don't forget this," he said. "You don't want to get cold."

Lucy grabbed the sweater and we walked home. Fast.

"Yowzer," I said. "When Chuckie spied the binoculars, I thought we were goners."

"Lucky for the noon whistle," Kyle said. "But too bad we were skunked. We didn't see a single suspicious thing."

"True, but we can look later this afternoon," Lucy said, putting on her sweater. She stuck her hands in her sweater pocket. "Hey! What's this?" She pulled out a box. A little box. She took off the lid. Inside were earrings. "These aren't mine," she said. "I don't even wear earrings! How did they get in my pocket?"

"CHUCKIE!" Kyle and I shouted together. "Computer chips!"

"Let's get back to headquarters," I said. "We can send these to the authorities."

We raced to Kyle's house and ran up the stairs to headquarters. As soon as we got there, Scarface made the sneezing sound.

"Scarface still has a cold, huh?" I asked.

"I guess so," said Kyle, lifting him out of his cage.

"*Mwiiip!*" sneezed Scarface.

Lucy and I wrote another report to *Alert!*

REPORT #2

Dear Alert!,

We just spied on the kid we told you about— Chuckie. There was nothing unusual on the premises. Chuckie was the same.

When we left Chuckie's, Lucy found these earrings in her pocket. They could have computer chips inside. Please inspect.

Detectively yours,
Scarface Detectives

Lucy folded the report and put it in an envelope with the earrings. Meanwhile, Kyle had been petting Scarface. Scarface bobbed up and down, up and down.

"How come you keep bobbing? Is something wrong?" Kyle asked Scarface. Then he held his hand out to pet him . . . *and Scarface puked in Kyle's hand!!*

"Yuck!" cried Kyle. "Yuck, yuck, yuck." He slimed the puke into the garbage and wiped off his hand. Then he got this worried look on his face. "Wow, Scarface, you must be sick."

Kyle looked at Lucy and me. "What if something terrible is wrong with him?"

I didn't tell Kyle what I'd noticed. I didn't

tell him that Scarface was acting differently (the bobbing, the puking) and that he looked weird, dopey . . . like he had brain fryout, too. I didn't remind him that the guy with the sewer worms in *Alien* had puked. But I had to wonder. Could parrots be abducted?

7

Something Stinks

A week later, Lucy and I were lying in the tall grass in the empty lot. I said, "I'm worried about Scarface."

"Because of his cold?" asked Lucy.

"Maybe it's a cold. But maybe it's something else," I said. "Sometimes he acts like his old self, and sometimes he acts dopey . . . just like Chuckie."

"You mean he has brain fryout, too?" She thought for a minute. "Maybe you're right. Last night I walked into headquarters with my huge flashlight on. When Scarface saw it, he went crazy. He squawked and fluttered and crashed into the side of his cage."

"*He's afraid of sudden bright lights!* Like an abducted person," I said. "We'd better keep an eye on him."

We picked some clover and started sucking the sweet parts out of it. I said, "Man, it sure has been easy to keep an eye on Chuckie, hasn't it?"

"No kidding," said Lucy. "He's everywhere. Remember when Kyle moved away, and we were on that soccer team, the Bruisers?"

"Yup," I said. "We weren't doing so hot, and then Chuckie laughed at us and said, 'You're nothing but a bunch of losers. You should change your name from the Bruisers to the *Losers!*'"

Lucy's eyes got skinny when she thought about it. "Yeah. And then we

wanted him on the team because he was
so big. But he made us PAY!"

"Four bucks a week," I said.

"And *then* he made us work, too. He
made us mow his lawn and collect bottles."

"He laughed at us."

"He sang the K-I-S-S-I-N-G song about
us."

I spit out the clover. The sweet part was
gone.

I pictured Chuckie's laughing face. I remembered the way food stuck in his teeth and he didn't even care, and his hair stuck up like nails and you could see his head skin through the spikes. I pictured his big, thick legs with motorcycle boots at the bottom of them, and then I saw . . .

. . . big, thick legs with motorcycle boots at the bottom of them. I gulped. It was Chuckie. For real.

I shielded my eyes against the sun and looked up at his mean face. But Chuckie didn't look mean. He looked almost . . . nice. And his teeth were clean.

"Hello, Willie," he said. "Hello, Lucille."

"Uh, hi," said Lucy.

"Do you mind if I join you?" he asked, sitting down.

"I guess not," I said. This was it. There were just two of us this time, Lucy and me. Two is a lot weaker than three. If Chuckie was himself, he'd try to trick us. If he was

mind-controlled, he'd attack us. I got ready to explode out of the grass and run for my life.

"Nice day," said Chuckie.

I bunched up tighter.

"Or is it too hot for you?" he asked. "Because if it's too hot, I could stand up and make some shade."

It would be easy to attack us if we were lying down and Chuckie was

standing up. "No!" I cried, jumping up. "I mean, it's fine like this." I've never taken karate, but I've watched TV shows about it. I got ready for a *hi-ya!* move.

"Do you think so, too, Lucille?" Chuckie asked.

"How come you keep calling me Lucille?" asked Lucy.

"I thought you might like it," said

Chuckie. "But I won't call you Lucille if you don't want me to. I'll call you anything you want. Well, I mean, *almost* anything. There probably are some things I wouldn't call you . . . unless you really wanted me to, and then I could."

Lucy leaned forward and eyeballed Chuckie's face. "Chuckie," she said. "Your face is red."

Chuckie stuck his hand on his face.

"Really?" he asked. "I'm sorry," he said. His face got redder. "Gotta go," he said . . . and took off in a flash. Boy, he sure could move fast for a big guy.

Lucy sniffed the air. "Pew!" she said. "Something stinks around here."

"It smells kind of sweet," I said. "Like flowers."

We figured it out at the same time. "IT'S COLOGNE!"

♦ 8 ♦

Magic Eight Ball

REPORT #3

Dear Alert!,

We've kept an eye on Chuckie, the kid who may have been abducted. Here's what we noticed:

1. He's everywhere.

2. When we aren't watching Chuckie, he's watching us.

3. He's wearing cologne.

That's all.

We're waiting for your instructions. We've been waiting a LONG TIME. Please write a.s.a.p.

Detectively yours,
Scarface Detectives

Now we were at headquarters. Waiting. Here's something I've noticed about spying. It's fun for a while. But then you want to *do* something.

That's how we were feeling now. We wanted to *do* something.

But we hadn't heard from the authorities yet.

I picked up the Magic Eight Ball. "Magic Eight Ball," I chanted in a hocus-pocus voice. "I want to know about Chuckie. Does he have brain fryout?"

The answer floated in the window. It is decidedly so.

Ha! Now we were getting somewhere. I tried again. "Magic Eight Ball, has Chuckie ever been abducted by aliens?"

The answer floated up. It is uncertain.

"Okay, then," I said. "Tell me what's wrong with Chuckie Herman."

I shook the Magic Eight Ball and concentrated hard. I waited for the answer to float up. It said, Ask again later.

I waited ten seconds. Now it was later. I asked it again. Yes. I shook it. My reply is no. I shook it. Outlook not so good. I shook it. Yes, definitely.

I stared at it, eyeball to eight ball, and

said, "Hey! Make up your mind!" Then I put it down. "This isn't a Magic Eight Ball. It's a magic *fake* ball."

Man, oh, man. It was really getting hard to wait. I looked at Lucy. She looked at me. Lucy looked at Kyle. He looked at me. Waiting is way harder than doing.

I jiggled my knee against the side of the desk. *Bonk bonk. Bonk bonk.* "I'm getting tired of waiting for *Alert!* to tell us what to do next."

Kyle bounced in his chair, squeaking the cushions. *Creak creak. Creak creak.* "Me, too. The aliens could be looking for another victim right now . . . and we're just sitting here."

Lucy tapped her pencil on the table. *Tap tap. Tap tap.* "Waiting is driving me nuts."

Bonk bonk. Creak creak. Tap tap.

"*Squaaaaawk!*" screeched Scarface.

Scarface. I'd been keeping an eye on

him, too. Sometimes he acted normal—squawky and bossy—other times he acted dopey and bobbed up and down. Sometimes he threw up. Sometimes he didn't. I'll tell you, I was plenty worried about our good old mascot.

But more than worried, I was bored. I felt like I had cartoonhead—that fuzzy way your head feels when you watch too much TV. Only I hadn't been watching TV. I wondered what there was to do at home. Probably nothing. But at least at home there was stuff to eat. "See you tomorrow," I said.

When I got home, I stacked a bunch of chocolate-chip cookies on the kitchen table. I poured a glass of milk. I ate a cookie. As I reached for another, Mom came in. She looked at my cookie stack.

"It looks like you have a lot of thinking to do," she said. "Do you want to tell me about it?"

"It's official detective business . . . " I said, "but maybe I *should* tell you. The magazine said to notify the authorities. And moms are kind of like authorities, aren't they?"

"Around here they are," said Mom.

First I told her about Scarface. She said Kyle should take him to the vet.

Then I told her about how funny Chuckie was acting and our theory that he had been abducted. She said, "It sounds like Chuckie's not acting like himself, all right. But there are lots of reasons for a person to act differently. Abduction is only one possibility."

"It *may* be only one possibility," I said. "But it *is* the best one."

"Why don't you ask him?" Mom asked.

"Are you kidding?" I said. "If he *was* abducted, he might be dangerous if he knew we were on to him. And if he *wasn't* abducted, he'd probably pound me."

"Maybe Chuckie really has changed. Maybe he wants to be friends," she said, and then she left.

Boy, Mom really didn't get Chuckie. Maybe she never knew any rotten kids when she was a girl. But she did have one good point. We had to find out for sure.

I ate another cookie.

There must be a way to figure out if Chuckie had been abducted. What we needed was proof. But how would we get it?

I ate another cookie.

I needed a plan.

I ate another cookie. Then I remembered how Scarface went crazy with the flashlight. That was it!

◆ 9 ◆

Chuckie Freaks

If Kyle had the best detective stuff, and I had the best food . . . Lucy had the best disguises. I decided to go to her house first. I rang the doorbell and walked in at the same time. But before I could tell her my plan, Lucy started talking.

"Scarface is sick!" she said. "He puked in Kyle's hand again."

"Do you think it's brain fryout?" I asked. "Do you think Scarface has sewer worms?"

"There's only one way to find out for sure about sewer worms, and that's to poke around in his parrot slime. Kyle and I figured there were two choices. One of *us* could poke around . . . or the vet could. Kyle took Scarface to the vet. He's there right now."

"Good choice," I agreed. "Man, I really hope Scarface is okay. But maybe it'll cheer up Kyle if we can prove that Chuckie was abducted," I said. "It just so happens I have a brilliant plan." And then I told her.

"That's the wildest plan I've ever heard," said Lucy. "It's so wild, it might work."

"I *am* Wild Willie," I reminded her.

We flipped a nickel to see who would be the alien. I won. We went to Lucy's disguise box. I wasn't sure what we were looking for. "What does an alien look like?" I asked. "The only pictures I've ever seen are fuzzy."

"That's because aliens are full of light.

Their body light makes the pictures fuzzy. That's why you need some kind of light if you're going to look like a real alien."

Lucy rummaged around in the box and pulled out some of those glow-in-the-dark rings, the kind we wear while we wait for fireworks on the Fourth of July. "I haven't used these yet," she said, "so they'll glow when they're snapped."

Next, I rummaged around in the box myself. When I spied green body makeup, I said, "Most aliens are green!" Then I spread the makeup on my arms and legs.

"And they have pale faces," said Lucy, smearing white makeup on my cheeks. She stood back and looked at me. "Well, you still look like you, only green . . . but if Chuckie was really abducted, he'll just go bonko and won't notice."

"And I'll look even better when I glow," I said hopefully.

Lucy said, "I'll get my stuff and meet you at Chuckie's house." We gave each other a good luck handshake, and then I walked to Chuckie's alone.

You know how plans seem real good when you first think of them? And they seem even better when you're with a friend? But when you're alone, your stomach starts to feel gross because then you're not so sure? That's how I felt. I didn't even need body paint to look green.

Chuckie was on his driveway, riding his skateboard. It was almost dark, so it wasn't hard to sneak past him and hide behind a bush. While I waited for Lucy, I went over the plan. Lucy would come with her big flashlight and hide behind another bush. She'd shine it on Chuckie. We'd make a spaceship noise. If Chuckie had been abducted before, he'd think it was a spaceship, landing. I'd activate my glow tubes and jump out of the bushes. Chuckie would think I was an alien, coming back for him.

Then he'd freak. He'd grab his head and scream. He'd run off somewhere to hide, like maybe under his bed. Then we'd have proof.

If Chuckie hadn't ever been abducted, he'd recognize me under the paint and I'd get pounded.

Pretty soon I heard leaves swishing. It was Lucy, hiding behind a bush near mine. She aimed the giant flashlight right at Chuckie's face and snapped it on. Man, was it bright! We both made the sound of a

spaceship landing, "ZZZZZHOOOOOOO-OOOOOOOARRRRR."

I snapped my glow tubes on and leaped out of the bushes. I was right about one thing, Chuckie freaked . . .

. . . only he didn't run for cover, he ran for me. In one millionth of a second he was flying through the air, straight for green little me.

"Pervert!" Chuckie yelled.

"*Aaaaaugh!*" I screamed.

BLOODGE! Chuckie landed on top of me.

I wanted to scream bloody murder, but I couldn't breathe. "*Hhhhh! Hhhhh!*" I gasped. I would have run for cover, but I was paralyzed. Chuckie pulled his giant arm back and got ready to sock me into outer space . . . when suddenly he stopped.

"Willie . . . ?" he asked. "Is that you?"

"Yes," I squeaked.

Then Chuckie looked behind the bush at Lucy. "Lucille?" he asked. "Are you all right?"

"Yes," Lucy said. "But how did you know I was here?"

"I saw you walk behind my bushes with your flashlight." Then Chuckie thumped his thick finger into my chest. "I thought *you* were some weirdo. I thought you were trying to hurt Lucille. What's going on here?"

Gulp.

"You'd better tell me the truth. *I'll know if you're lying,*" he said.

So I spilled. "We thought you'd been abducted by aliens. We thought if we shot this light at you and you freaked, then we'd know if you'd been abducted. L-l-like on the TV show."

"ARE YOU NUTS?" Chuckie shouted. "Excuse me for shouting, Lucille. WHAT MADE YOU THINK I'D BEEN ABDUCT-ED?"

"You weren't acting like your regular self," explained Lucy.

In my life, a lot of things have surprised me. Last Christmas, I got detective stuff and jumping shoes and not a single piece of clothing. That was a surprise. When Lucy turned out to be a bud, even though she's a girl, that was a surprise.

When I found a rock in my salad garden and I thought it was an Indian arrowhead and I took it to the museum, and it was . . . that was a big surprise.

Nothing, however, surprised me as much as this.

Chuckie said, "Thanks."

Like a Watermelon

On the way to headquarters, I sniffed my shirt. It stank of cologne. Chuckie's. I asked, "How come Chuckie said thanks? He never says thanks."

"Yeah. He's still acting like he has brain fryout. If he wasn't abducted, what's going on?" Lucy said.

"Beats me," I said. "Anyway, I'm starting to change my mind about Chuckie. Maybe he's rotten, but not rotten all the way through."

"Maybe Chuckie's like a watermelon," Lucy said. "Tough on the outside, but sweet inside."

"Maybe," I said. Maybe Chuckie was sweet. *Maybe.* But I was still going to be careful. "Anyway," I said. "Even if he's part-nice, it doesn't explain why he's suddenly acting differently."

When we got to Kyle's, he opened the door. Scarface was on his shoulder. *"Hello!"* said Scarface.

"You'll never guess what!" everybody said at once.

Then Kyle looked at me. "How come you're dressed funny?" he asked.

"You first," I said.

Kyle covered Scarface's head with his hand, so he couldn't hear.

"Hey, whatsa matter? Hello. Hello." Scarface muttered from under Kyle's hand.

Kyle whispered. "He loves me."

"Of course he does," said Lucy. "You're pals."

"No," said Kyle. "Not pal-love. The other kind. Scarface is a girl."

"Huh?"

Kyle uncovered Scarface's head. "That weird way he's been acting . . . I mean *she.* That weird way? It's l-o-v-e."

"What about the sneezing?" I asked.

"They're *kisses!*" Kyle said. "And I have no idea of how she learned to do that."

"Maybe from Lorraine," said Lucy. "But what about the puking?"

"It's called regurgitation. It's what birds do when they l-o-v-e somebody," Kyle said.

"Well, then, it's a good thing you don't have an eagle for a pet," I said.

"*Braaaack!*" shrieked Scarface.

"One more thing," I said. "Scarface went bonko when . . . she . . . saw bright lights. How come?"

"The vet said lots of animals act that way when there's a sudden light," Kyle explained. "Even when they haven't been abducted." He puffed his chest up like a parrot. "The vet also said I have a pretty smart bird. African Greys are the smartest parrots and the best talkers. But of course I already knew that."

Then he said, "Now tell me why you're dressed funny."

We did.

"So we still don't know why Chuckie's acting weird?"

"Nothing for sure," said Lucy. "But I have my suspicions."

I had suspicions, too. But they were too horrible to say out loud.

"Well . . . ?" said Kyle.

Lucy looked at me, and I looked at Lucy. I knew that she knew that I knew. But she didn't say it, either.

There was a knock on the door.

"*Hello!*" said Scarface. "*Come in come in come in.*"

Kyle opened the door, and his mom stuck her hand in. "Mail for Scarface Detectives."

Scarface snatched the envelope and flew with it to her perch. In one second, she had ripped it open with her sharp beak.

"Wow!" said Lucy. "I guess Loraine

taught him—I mean her—to open mail."
She took the envelope from Scarface
and took a look. "Guys! It's from *Alert!*"

Dear Detectives,

*The tests on the earrings were negative.
There were no computer chips.*
*You've got yourselves a real problem there.
It's hard to tell if someone has been abducted.
Brain fryout usually has one of two causes:*
1. Abduction

2. Love

Did you say the subject has been wearing cologne?

If we can be of further assistance, please write.

> *Detectively yours,*
> *Alert!*

Lucy slumped in a chair. "Ohhhhhh." She held her head like she was dizzy. She moaned again and mumbled, "Chuckie . . . loves . . . me . . ."

Scarface flew to her shoulder. *"Awww. Poor baby!"*

I didn't know what to say. Lucy was right. Chuckie had brain fryout for Lucy!

"Gross," said Kyle. Then he shrugged. "But things could be worse."

"They could?" asked Lucy.

"Sure. My cousin, Stu, says he's a chick

magnet. He says chicks love him. 'But hey,' Stu says. 'It's not so bad. Love sorta rumbles around for a while. And then it passes. Like gas.'"

◆ 11 ◆

Watermelon or Gas?

It was two weeks later. If this was love, it sure was a lot like gas, just like Kyle's cousin Stu said.

Chuckie followed Lucy everywhere. He picked her flowers. He called her Lucille. He was nice. The whole thing made all of us twitchy . . . especially Lucy.

We were at my house, hiding from Chuckie.

"Remember the good old days, when Chuckie was really rotten?" said Kyle.

"Yeah," I said. "I thought there were some things in life that you could really count on."

"I don't know," said Lucy. "Sometimes people surprise you. Maybe Chuckie really *is* sweet like a watermelon."

Kyle's mouth flew open. My eyeballs popped out of my head. "WHAT?!" we said together.

"Lucy, you aren't getting brain fryout, too, are you?" I asked.

Lucy's eyes snapped. "No!" she said.

But I wasn't so sure. Watermelon or gas? Which one was it? Would Chuckie *stay* sweet on Lucy like a watermelon, or would it pass like gas? And what would happen to Lucy? Would she get brain fry-out for Chuckie?

The Magic Eight Ball was no help either. Every time I shook it, the same answer floated up: Reply hazy. Try again.

"I think it's broken," said Kyle.

Maybe Chuckie was broken, too. Maybe he'd always be stuck on Lucy. Maybe, even, someday they'd get . . .

But no. That was too horrible to think about.

"Come on," Lucy said. "Let's go outside."

"Chuckie will be out there," I reminded her.

Lucy sighed. "I know."

He was out there. "Hi, guys!" he said. He skidded to a stop on his dirt bike.

"Hi, Chuckie," Lucy said.

"Hey, I have a new game," he said. "It's a hitting contest."

Gulp.

"I don't want to play," I said. "I don't like getting hit."

"Don't worry," said Chuckie. "Because it's a contest to see who can hit the *softest!*"

"I don't know . . . " said Lucy.

Chuckie looked sad.

"Well, I guess it would be okay," she said.

Chuckie held out his hand. "I'll let you go first. But remember," he said, "it's a contest to see who can hit the softest. And you only have one chance."

Lucy hit first. She steadied one hand

with the other. She touched down on Chuckie's hand with her pinkie. Like a feather.

"Okay. Now it's my turn," Chuckie said. Then he creamed Lucy's hand.

"Ow! That was *hard*," said Lucy. "I thought you said it was a *soft* hitting contest!"

"I know," he said. "It was. AND YOU WON!"

Then Chuckie laughed. "Har har har!" His teeth had food stuck in them. And I noticed his hair was spiked again.

Lucy was boiling mad. Little knives shot from her eyes. "Chuckie Herman, you scum. You're nothing but a big old bully."

"I know," said Chuckie, snorting. He jumped on his dirt bike and tore off.

We grinned like crazy. Stu was right about love, after all. It passes. Chuckie was back to his good old rotten self. In this world, it's nice to count on some things.

We went back to headquarters and put our feet up. Scarface flew around. *"Stick 'em up, suckers!"* she screamed. *"Pow pow pow pow pow."* If Scarface was still in l-o-v-e with Kyle, she wasn't acting like it now. Maybe her brain fryout had passed, too.

Ahhh. Things were back to normal. Chuckie was a bully. Me, Scarface, Kyle, and Lucy were buds. We had our own headquarters. And now, there was one more mystery solved.

"Isn't life the greatest?" I asked. Then I picked up the Magic Eight Ball . . . just to see if it was working again. An answer floated up. Yes, definitely.

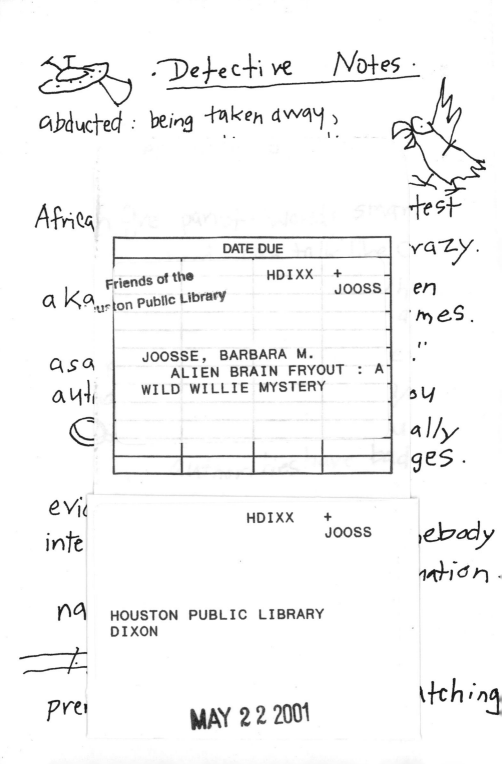

·Detective Notes·

abducted : being taken away⸴

Africa ... test
... razy.

a Ka ... en
... mes.
..."

as a ...
aut ... by
... ally
... ges.

evi ...
inte ... ebody
... ation.

na ...

pre ... tching